Your Special NAME

Amanda McDonald Sheff

Amanda McDonald Sheff

WestBow Press books may be ordered through booksellers or by contacting:

WestBow Press
A Division of Thomas Nelson & Zondervan
1663 Liberty Drive
Bloomington, IN 47403
www.westbowpress.com
844-714-3454

 @your_special_name

www.yourspecialname.me

Interior Image Credit: Vidya Vasudevan

ISBN: 978-1-6642-1439-2 (sc)
ISBN: 978-1-6642-1601-3 (hc)
ISBN: 978-1-6642-1440-8 (e)

Library of Congress Control Number: 2020923870

Printed in the Unbited States of America.

WestBow Press rev. date: 03/08/2021

WESTBOW
P R E S S®
A DIVISION OF THOMAS NELSON
& ZONDERVAN

To my three special angels, Billy Mac,
Samuel and Stella Grace.
May you always respect this beautiful earth,
love others, and love yourselves.

I have a name. You have a name. We
all have a *SPECIAL* name.

While it is true that we are all different and unique,
what we have in common is a *SPECIAL* name.

A name that was given to you at your
birth or maybe a few days later.
A name that was in an exciting and memorable
dream or unexpectedly greater.

How on this beautiful earth did you
get your *SPECIAL* name?
Let's think together of all the possibilities.

Maybe it's Tom, Dom, Sean, or Juan?
No? I know!

Billy, Willy, Lilly, or Hilly?
Or even Mac, Jack, Zack, or Novak?

Surely, your SPECIAL name is Stella, Ariella, Bella, or Marcella.

It's most definitely Alexa, Rebecca, Asia, or Jada!
Or maybe it's Grayson, Addison, Houston, or Mason?

I bet it's Cynthia, Maria,
Kecia, or Rashida.
Am I close with Chalondra,
Tamara, Zahra, or Barbara?

Or, quite possibly, it's Gianna, Anika, Naava, or Fernanda.
What aboooooooooooooout Kerlin, Merlin, Harlyn, or Marlin?

I've got it! It's a doubly SPECIAL name like Sophia-Grace, Tucker Joe, John Paul, or Scarlett Rose. Or perhaps Jayden-Lee, Jack Thomas, Lacey Mae, or Lilly Ann?

HELGA

Zaylee

Claire

Alva

Linda

Sarah

Rosalind

Catalina

Noah

Abigail

Angeliki

Lucia

Jamie Lynn

Alice

SHAURYA

MIKHAEL LUCA

Mark Paul

Venus

Magnus

LAURA BETH

SOLEIL DIEGO

ANNE MARIE

NAVYA Ishan

ALIYAH Ioannis

Wyatt
RUBY
RAE
MOHAMMED
Ryder
Miyu
Auburn
Elijah
Willow
Mary Elizabeth
Agnus
BROOKLYN
Xander
Billy Joe

Daisy

Fernanda

LUNA

Kathy Lee

PAYTON

John-Grey

Brinley

Easton

Rashad

Pearl

Quinten

Asher

VAUGHN

Zuri

Juho Arsalan

Is it possible you were named after a
state or your mom's favorite flower?
How about an animal or the
largest city tower?

I am confident you were named after
your **GROOVY** great aunt Jo.
Or maybe from your adored grandpa, who lives in Idaho.

It could have been a planet,
a star, or the moon.
It was quite possibly
a last-minute pick in
your delivery room.

Were you named after a special fruit that so many of us love?
A diamond in the rough or the sunshine up above?

I guarantee your name comes from your
dad's favorite styling car. Or maybe where
your parents met at a chic little bar.
Did you take your name from your grandma or grandpa?
Or sentimentally from your mom's sweet cousin Samantha?

Do you think it's from a tradition driven family
and their wildly famous sports team?
Or a wonderful name idea that came
to your big brother in a dream?

With so many possibilities, there is one thing that's for sure.
Your name was given out of LOVE.
To the moon and back, so pure!

Two *special* people, or many more for that matter,
chose your SPECIAL name for all the world to chatter.

NORTH
AMERICA

Atlantic
Ocean

EUROP

Afric

SOUTH
AMERICA

Pacific
Ocean

And if someone can't pronounce or process
your name on the first, second, or THIIIIIIIRD
try, do not fret. Just gently remind them
their name is *SPECIAL*, like yours and mine.

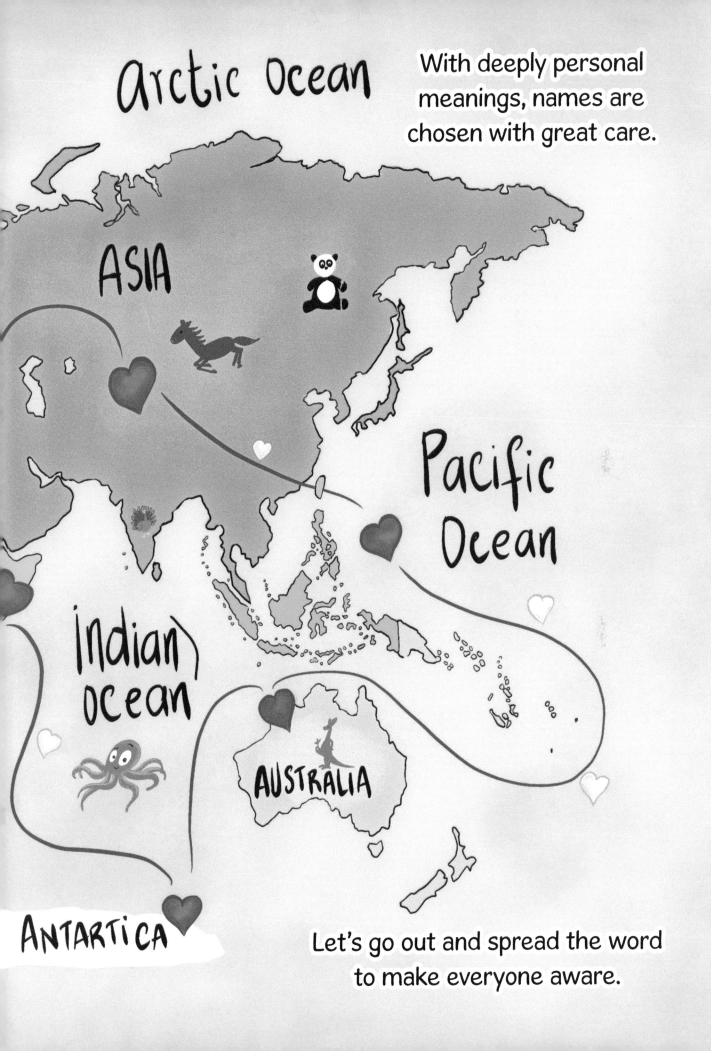

So go and be yourself!

State "_____"
loud, because your name is *SUPER SPECIAL*
and you should feel very, VERY proud!